9/02 UNIVERSITY OF
WOLVERHAMPTON
ENTERPRISE LTD.
LR/LEND/001

D1580500

WP 0499375 6
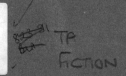
TP
FICTION

ALL JOIN IN

QUENTIN BLAKE

POLYTECHNIC LIBRARY
WOLVERHAMPTON

ACC. 499375   GRADE

829
.3
BLA   TP

15. JAN 1992   WL

PICTURE BOOK

JONATHAN CAPE
LONDON

Other books by Quentin Blake

PATRICK
JACK AND NANCY
ANGELO
SNUFF
MISTER MAGNOLIA
QUENTIN BLAKE'S NURSERY RHYME BOOK
THE STORY OF THE DANCING FROG
MRS ARMITAGE ON WHEELS
QUENTIN BLAKE'S ABC

In This Book

All Join In

The Hooter Song

Nice Weather for Ducks

Sliding

Sorting Out the Kitchen Pans

Bedtime Song

All Join In

Important Message
YOU CAN JOIN IN
TOO

for Linda

All Join In

When Sandra plays the trumpet
it makes a lovely sound

And Mervyn on his drum-kit
can be heard for
miles around

Stephanie is brilliant
when she plays the violin

But the very best of all is when
we ALL JOIN IN

When Amy throws a tantrum
it is wonderful to see

And when Eric starts his wailing
there is noise enough for three

When Bernard kicks the dustbin
it really makes a din

But the very best of all is when
we ALL JOIN IN

The Hooter Song

When William's in his study
   and his thoughts are very deep
We come and help him concentrate —

We go BEEP-BEEP BEEP-BEEP

When Lilian sings a sad song
  and we think she's going to weep
We like to come and cheer her up —

We go BEEP-BEEP BEEP-BEEP

When Oscar's on the sofa
   and he's curled up fast asleep
We know he likes a serenade —

We go BEEP-BEEP BEEP-BEEP

Nice Weather for Ducks

We're all off to the river
   along the muddy track
And we're joining in the Duck Song
   QUACK QUACK QUACK

We each have our umbrella
   and our wellies and our mack
And we're joining in the Duck Song
   QUACK QUACK QUACK

We don't care if it's raining
and the sky is murky black —
We're joining in the Duck Song
QUACKQUACKQUACKQUACKQUACK

Sliding

It's cold and wet and dark outside
In here we'll have a lovely slide
All down the banisters —

WHEEEE!

It's large and grey and lots of fun
We're sliding down it one by one
All down the elephant —

WHEEEEEE!

We're in the wind and sun and snow
Let's see how fast our sledge will go
All down the mountainside —

WHEEEEEEE!

BUMP!

Sorting Out the Kitchen Pans

We're sorting out the Kitchen Pans
DING DONG BANG
Sorting out the Kitchen Pans
BING BONG CLANG

Sorting out the Kitchen Pans
TING BANG DONG
Sorting out the Kitchen Pans
CLANG DING BONG

Sorting out the Kitchen Pans
DONG DANG BONG
TING TANG BING BANG
CLANG DING

OW

Bedtime Song

The stars above are glittering
The moon is gleaming bright
And noisy cats are singing songs
Down in the yard tonight
MIAOW WOW WOW
WOW WOW

People in their dressing-gowns
In houses far and near
Are leaning from their window sills
They're horrified to hear
MIAOW WOW WOW
WOW WOW

But we don't want a lullaby
   We prefer a din
Noisy cats are what we like —
   All join in!
MIAOW WOW WOW
        WOW WOW
            WOW WOW

All Join In

When we're cleaning up the house
We ALL JOIN IN

When we're trying to catch a mouse
We ALL JOIN IN

When we've got some tins of paint
We ALL JOIN IN

And when Granny's going to faint
We ALL JOIN IN

And if Ferdinand decides to make
        a chocolate fudge banana cake
                What do we do? For goodness sake!

We
ALL JOIN IN

All Join In
First published 1990
Text and illustrations © Quentin Blake 1990
Jonathan Cape Ltd, 20 Vauxhall Bridge Road, London SW1V 2SA

A CIP catalogue record for this book
is available from the British Library

ISBN 0-244-02770-0

Printed in Italy by
Arti Grafiche Motta S.p.A., Milan